An I Can Read Book®

WIZARD and WART

STORY BY **JANICE LEE SMITH**
PICTURES BY **PAUL MEISEL**

HarperCollins*Publishers*

To all the Great Great-Grand Smiths!
Nichole and Kaelee
Kristie, Kody, and Kacey
Shawna, Aaron, and Kaitland
Rebel, Brett, and Wesley
—J.L.S.

For David Schorr
—P.M.

Wizard and Wart
Text copyright © 1994 by Janice Lee Smith
Illustrations copyright © 1994 by Paul Meisel
Printed in the U.S.A. All rights reserved.
Typography by Alicia Mikles

Library of Congress Cataloging-in-Publication Data
Smith, Janice Lee, date
  Wizard and Wart/ story by Janice Lee Smith ; pictures by Paul Meisel.
    p.   cm. — (An I can read book)
  Summary: When Wizard and his dog Wart advertise their magic business, they have some problems with several lovesick customers.
  ISBN 0-06-022960-8. — ISBN 0-06-022961-6 (lib. bdg.)
  [1. Wizards—Fiction. 2. Magic—Fiction. 3. Animals—Fiction.] I. Meisel, Paul, ill. II. Title. III. Series.
PZ7.S6499Wi   1994   92-41170
[E]—dc20   CIP
                                                                               AC

1   2   3   4   5   6   7   8   9   10
❖
First Edition

Contents

Moving In

The Wizard moved into his new home

with Zounds, his bird,

and Wart, his dog.

6

"We have lots of room," said Wizard.

"We can do hocus in the front

and pocus in the back!"

"And then take naps in the middle,"

said Wart.

Wizard put out his sign.

"Just watch, Wart!" he said.

"People with problems

will zoom to our door."

They waited all morning.

Nobody zoomed.

"Maybe we need a new sign,"

Wizard said.

"Maybe," said Wart.

10

Wizard
and
Wart
NOW OPEN

We fix problems.

They waited all afternoon.

Nobody came.

"Now," Wart said, "we are the ones

with problems."

"A curse and worse!" Wizard said.

"I'm an out-of-work Wizard."

"And I'm an out-of-work Wart,"

said Wart.

That night Wizard stayed up and read

Great-Uncle Gizard's books.

"Now," he said,

"I know just what to do."

"A spiffy spell?" asked Wart.

"A new brew?"

"Nope," Wizard said with a yawn.

"We need to advertise."

The next day Wizard was busy

with his kettle.

"It smells great to advertise,"

Wart said.

"Wart!" said Wizard.

"This is how stew smells.

We will advertise tonight,

but now I am hungry for stew."

"That's even better," said Wart.

They ate stew

and waited for nighttime.

Wizard told Wart some Wizard jokes.

Wart told Wizard some Wart jokes.

16

"Okay," Wizard said,

"now it's time to advertise."

a r d

w a r t

we fix problems

"*That* should do it!"

Wizard told Wart.

The Snake

Early the next morning,

there was a knock at the door.

Wart opened it and looked high.

Then he looked low.

Then lower.

There was a snake.

"My name is Floyd,"

he said.

"Slither on in," said Wart.

"Slime into a chair."

"You are our first case!"

said Wizard.

"Tell me your troubles."

22

23

"I'm a snake," Floyd said.

"You hate being a snake,"

said Wizard.

"Who could blame you?"

"I like being a snake," said Floyd,

"but I'm in love with a rabbit.

I want you to turn her into a snake."

"That is a rotten idea," said Wizard.

"It is a great idea," said Floyd.

"She would make a great snake.

I can see it in her eyes."

"Sounds risky," said Wizard.

"It is true love," said Floyd.

Wizard looked worried,

but he hocused and pocused.

26

"Two toad rumps and kangaroo,"

he sang.

"All will make a tasty stew."

"Good grief!" Wart said

and turned green.

"That should do the trick,"

said Wizard.

"Thanks," Floyd said.

"You won't be sorry."

"I think I'm going to be sorry,"

said Wizard.

"I'm already sorry,"

said Wart.

29

The Rabbit

Early the next morning,

there was a knock at the door.

32

Wart looked high.

Then he looked low.

Then lower.

"You again?" he said.

"Who again?" asked the snake.

"Are you a new you?" asked Wart.

Wizard
and
Wart

"Yesterday," the snake said sadly,

"I was a cute rabbit named Wanda.

Then the farmer started yelling

'Snake! Snake!'

I hate snakes.

I tried to run,

but I could only slither!"

"Tragic magic," said Wizard.

"It got worse," cried Wanda.

"Last night a snake named Floyd
brought me a rose.

He said it was true love."

"That is what he told us," Wart said.

"Yuck!" said Wanda.

Snakes

38

"Floyd said you changed me
into a snake," Wanda said.
"So you can just change me back
into a rabbit again!"
"I don't know," said Wizard.
"Now!" yelled Wanda.

39

Wizard hocused and pocused.

He hopped and bopped.

"Anything else?" Wizard asked.

"As a matter of fact," Wanda said,

"I'm in love."

"Yikes!" cried Wart.

"He is a cat now," said Wanda,

"but he would make a great rabbit.

I can see it in his eyes."

"That is a bad idea," said Wizard.

"It is a great idea," said Wanda.

"Besides, you owe me."

"I could make you a cat instead," Wizard said.

"I have already been a snake today!" yelled Wanda.

"Right," said Wizard.

"Double yikes!" said Wart.

A Snake and Two Rabbits

Early the next morning,

there was a knock at the door.

"I am not going to open it,"

said Wart.

"Open it," said Wizard.

Wart looked high.

There was a tall rabbit.

Wart looked low.

There was Wanda.

"A hare pair," Wart said.

He looked lower.

There was a snake.

"Not funny," said Floyd.

They all came in and started yelling.

"That's enough!" said Wizard.

"Even a Wizard has his limits!"

"So does a Wart," said Wart.

Wizard hocused and pocused.

He fussed and fumed.

Suddenly three warthogs stood

where the other animals had been.

The tall warthog looked at Wanda.

"You are the warthog
of my heart," he said.

"Cut it out!" yelled Floyd.

"I saw her first."

Wizard hocused a little extra.

There was a knock at the door.

A new warthog stood there.

"I was just passing by,"

she told Wart,

"and I felt an urge to drop in."

"Warthog of *my* heart!" cried Floyd.

55

All the warthogs looked happy

and in love.

You could see it in their eyes.

"Good grief!" Wart said

as he pushed them out the door.

"Also, good-bye and good luck!

The next time," he told Wizard,

"choose something besides warthogs!

No animal named Wart

should be that ugly!"

Then they looked out the door.

"It pays to advertise," said Wart.

"Look at that line."

First in line was a snake.

Wizard shut the door quickly.

"We worked hard," he told Wart.

"Now it's time for a vacation."

"Are we going to the mountains?"
Wart asked.

"No," said Wizard, "the beach,

where there are no snakes."

"Vamoose!" Wizard yelled.

"That's a magic word,

when you need to hurry!"

How to Vamoose

63

There was a knock at the door,

but it was too late.

Wizard and Wart were already gone.

ER
SMITH   SMITH, JANICE LEE

          WIZARD AND WART

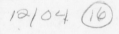

12/04 (16)